MISTER DOG

The Dog
Who Belonged to Himself

By Margaret Wise Brown

Pictures by Garth Williams

A GOLDEN BOOK, NEW YORK
Western Publishing Company, Inc., Racine, Wisconsin 53404

MARGARET WISE BROWN is one of the best-known and most prolific authors of books for children. Her sensitive, lively, tender, and often amusing stories have delighted both youngsters and their parents for generations. At one point in her career, Margaret Wise Brown decided to stop writing. Fortunately, she could not stop, and eventually she published more than eighty-five books. Among them are many well-loved Golden Books, including such enduring favorites as *Home for a Bunny, The Sailor Dog,* and *The Friendly Book.*

Born in New York, GARTH WILLIAMS had an extensive art education and early career interests in architecture, theatrical scenery design, oil painting, poster design, and sculpture. In 1945, he illustrated his first children's book, *Stuart Little.* Since then, his imaginative, endearing art work has enhanced more than fifty children's books. In addition to the Margaret Wise Brown books listed above, Garth Williams illustrated *Three Bedtime Stories, My Big Golden Counting Book, The Tiny Golden Library,* and many other popular Golden Books.

ONCE upon a time there was a funny dog
named Crispin's Crispian. He was named
Crispin's Crispian because—

he belonged to himself.

In the mornings, he woke himself up and he went
to the icebox and gave himself some bread and milk.
He was a funny old dog. He liked strawberries.

Then he took himself for a walk. And he went
wherever he wanted to go.

But one morning he didn't know where he
wanted to go.

"Just walk and sooner or later you'll get somewhere,"
he said to himself.

Soon he came to a country where there were
lots of dogs. They barked at him and he
barked back. Then they all played together.

But he still wanted to go somewhere, so he walked on until he came to a country where there were lots of cats and rabbits.

The cats and rabbits jumped in the air and ran. So Crispian jumped in the air and ran after them.

He didn't catch them because he ran bang into
a little boy.

"Who are you and who do you belong to?"
asked the little boy.

"I am Crispin's Crispian and I belong to myself,"
said Crispian. "Who and what are you?"

"I am a boy," said the boy, "and I belong
to myself."

"I am so glad," said Crispin's Crispian.
"Come and live with me."

Then they went to a butcher shop — ''to get his poor

dog a bone,'' Crispian said.

Now, since Crispin's Crispian belonged to himself,
he gave himself the bone and trotted home with it.

And the boy's little boy bought a big lamb chop
and a bright green vegetable and trotted home with
Crispin's Crispian.

Crispin's Crispian lived in a two-story doghouse in
a garden. And in his two-story doghouse, he had a
little fur living room with a warm fire that crackled
all winter and went out in the summer.

His house was always warm. His house had a chimney
for the smoke to go out. And upstairs there was
a little bedroom with a bed in it and a place for his leash
and a pillow under which he hid his bones.

And there was plenty of room in his house for the boy
to live there with him.

Crispian had a little kitchen upstairs in his two-story doghouse where he fixed himself a good dinner three times a day because he liked to eat. He liked steaks and chops and roast beef and chopped meat and raw eggs.

This evening he made a bone soup with lots of meat in it. He gave some to the boy, and the boy liked it. The boy didn't give Crispian his chop bone, but he put some of his bright green vegetable in the soup.

And what did Crispian do with his dinner?

Did he put it in his stomach?

Yes, indeed.

He chewed it up and swallowed it into his
little fat stomach.

And what did the little boy do with his dinner?

Did he put it in his stomach?

Yes, indeed.

He chewed it up and swallowed it into his
little fat stomach.

Crispin's Crispian was a *conservative*. He liked
everything at the right time—

    dinner at dinner time,

    lunch at lunchtime,

    breakfast in time for breakfast,

    and sunrise at sunrise,

    and sunset at sunset.

    And at bedtime—

At bedtime, he liked everything in its own place—

    the cup in the saucer,

    the chair under the table,

    the stars in the heavens,

    the moon in the sky,

    and himself in his own little bed.

And then what did he do?

Then he curled in a warm little heap and went to
sleep. And he dreamed his own dreams.

That was what the dog who belonged to himself did.

And what did the boy who belonged to himself do?

The boy who belonged to himself curled in a
warm little heap and went to sleep. And he dreamed
his own dreams.

That was what the boy who belonged to himself did.

GOOD NIGHT

AND

SWEET DREAMS.